RUSSELL
Rides Again

He went over to Jeremy.

"Hi," he said. It was funny to see his old friend in this new classroom.

"Hi, R-u-s-s-e-l-l," Jeremy spelled out.

He looked down at his own necklace. It had different letters on it.

"Ms. Cassedy said we had to wear these so she would know who we are," he told Russell.

"That's silly," said Russell. "We already know who we are. I'm Russell and you're Jeremy," he said. Then he had an idea. "Let's trade necklaces. Then we can pretend that I am Jeremy and you are Russell."

Jeremy laughed. That sounded like a good game to him.

"Don't tell anyone who you really are," said Russell. "And I won't tell anyone, either."

Johanna Hurwitz

RUSSELL
Rides Again

Illustrated by Lillian Hoban

A BEECH TREE PAPERBACK BOOK
New York

For Eve, Maurice, Claire, and David Posada
And a thousand afternoons
in Riverside Park

The Library of Congress has cataloged the Morrow Junior Books edition
of *Russell Rides Again* as follows:
Hurwitz, Johanna. Russell rides again. Summary: The adventures of Russell,
his family, and friends, as he gets ready to celebrate his sixth birthday.
ISBN 0-688-04628-2 (trade)
ISBN 0-688-04629-0 (lib. bdg.)
1. Children's stories, America. [1. Family life—Fiction.] I. Hoban, Lillian, ill.
II. Title. PZ7.H9574Ru 1985 [E] 85-7287

1 3 5 7 9 10 8 6 4 2
First Beech Tree Edition, 1999
ISBN 0-688-16665-2

Contents

Snow White
and the Seven Bears

Russell Michaels was five years old. He lived
with his parents and his little sister Elisa in an
apartment in New York City. Russell's friends
Teddy and Nora lived in the same apartment
building.

When June came, Russell graduated from
the Sunshine Nursery School. On the last day

1

of school there was a party. Everyone ate cup-cakes and ice cream, even though it was still morning. It was the first time Russell had ever eaten ice cream before lunch. He hoped they would eat ice cream every morning in the new kindergarten class he would go to in September.

"I will be in Teddy's class!" Russell told his mother.

"In September, when you are in kindergarten, Teddy will be in first grade," Mrs. Michaels explained. "He has finished kindergarten."

It wasn't fair. No matter how hard Russell tried, he was never able to catch up.

His mother reminded him that since his birthday was a month before Teddy's, there would be four weeks every year when both boys would be the same age. But it was still a long, long time until his birthday came again.

That afternoon, Russell, Teddy, and Nora were playing together. Teddy and Nora's grandpa was visiting, too.

"Kindergarten is fun," Teddy told Russell. "You will like it."

"Kindergarten is easy," Nora said. "First grade is easy, too. But second grade is hard. Wait till you get to second grade. Then you'll see."

Second grade seemed much too far away for Russell to worry about now. He was thinking about what they should do today.

"Let's watch TV," Russell suggested.

"I don't want to," said Teddy.

"Do you know that when I was a little boy, we didn't have television?" Teddy's grandpa said.

"No television?" said Russell. "Then how did you watch your programs?"

"We couldn't," said Grandpa. "We listened to the radio. We would close our eyes and imagine what everything looked like."

Nora and Teddy and Russell all closed their eyes.

"I can't see anything," Russell said. "It's dark."

"Come sit with me here on the sofa," said Grandpa. "I'll tell you a story. You can close your eyes and imagine it."

"Oh, yes," said Nora. "Make up a story for us."

"No," said Russell. "I want to hear about Snow White and the Seven Bears."

" 'Snow White and the Seven Bears'?" Nora laughed. "There's no such story. You mean 'Snow White and the Seven Dwarfs.' "

"Nora's right," said Teddy. "You're wrong, Russell."

"No," Russell insisted. "I want to hear about Snow White and the Seven Bears."

"Dwarfs," said Nora.

"Dwarfs," said Teddy.

"Bears," shouted Russell. "I want a story about bears."

"How about 'Goldilocks and the Three Bears'?" said Nora. "That's a story about bears."

"I want to hear 'Snow White and the Seven Bears,' " said Russell, trying hard not to cry.

4

"Wait a minute," said Grandpa. "I think I know that one. It goes like this.

"Once upon a time, when Snow White was living with the Seven Dwarfs, she went for a walk in the forest. She started to pick some flowers to bring home to them. All at once she heard a voice. 'What are you doing, little girl?' said the voice."

"That sounds like the wolf who met Little Red Riding Hood in the forest," said Nora. "That's what he said."

"No," said Grandpa. "It wasn't a wolf."

"Was it a bear?" Russell guessed.

"How did you know?" asked Grandpa. "It certainly was. The bear was very small and he was lost. 'I went for a walk all by myself,' he said, 'and now I can't find my way home.' Snow White was a very kind girl. She had some chewing gum in her pocket, and she gave it to the little bear. 'Do you live with a medium-size mama and a great big papa bear?' she asked.

" 'Yes,' said the little bear. 'And I also live with my baby sister and my three brother bears. We are quadruplets.' "

"What are quadruplets?" asked Russell.

"They're like twins," said Grandpa, "but there are four of them instead of two."

"Stop interrupting," said Nora. "What happened then?"

"Well, Snow White said to the little bear, 'I'll try to help you find your way home, but I don't want to get lost myself.'

" 'Couldn't you leave a trail in the forest?' asked the little bear. 'I once saw some children do that. They left a trail of pebbles.' "

"That was 'Hansel and Gretel,' " said Russell.

"Stop interrupting," said Teddy.

"Snow White felt in her other pocket. There was a package of M&M candies. So, as she walked through the woods, she left a trail of green and yellow and orange candies. Pretty soon they came to a small house. 'Do

7

you live there?' she asked the little bear.

" 'No,' said the bear. 'Bears don't live in houses. We live in caves.' "

"What about 'Goldilocks and the Three Bears'?" asked Teddy. "Those bears lived in a house."

"Funny you should mention that," said Grandpa. "Because who do you think lived in this house?"

"Who?" asked Russell.

"Goldilocks!" said Grandpa. "She came out of the door and she saw Snow White and the little bear. 'Where are you going?' she asked.

" 'We're looking for the home of this little bear,' Snow White told her.

" 'Can I come with you?' asked Goldilocks.

" 'Sure,' they said.

"So the three of them kept on walking. Pretty soon they came upon a little girl in a red cape. She was picking flowers just like Snow White had been doing a little while before.

" 'Hi,' Snow White called to her. 'Who are you picking flowers for?'

"The little girl looked at Snow White, but she didn't answer.

" 'Are you shy?' asked Snow White. 'My name is Snow White.'

"Still the little girl didn't answer. 'What's the matter?' asked the little bear. 'Don't you want to be friends with us?'

"The little girl nodded her head. 'My parents told me not to speak to strangers,' she whispered. 'The last time I spoke to a stranger, I got into big trouble.' "

"That was the wolf," whispered Teddy.

" 'You won't get into any trouble with us,' Snow White promised. 'We're helping this little bear find his way home. Do you want to come along?' The little girl in the red cape nodded. Along the path they went, first Snow White dropping green and yellow and orange candies, then the little bear chewing his gum. After him Goldilocks came skipping along and, following behind, still holding her flowers, came the little girl in the red cape."

"Little Red Riding Hood," said Nora.

"Stop interrupting," said Teddy.

"They hadn't gone very far before they met a brother and sister who were playing in the forest. They were picking berries and eating them. 'What kind of berries are those?' asked Snow White.

" 'I think they are raspberries,' answered the girl.

" 'No, Gretel,' said the boy. 'They are blackberries.'

" 'Perhaps they are black raspberries,' said Snow White. 'Could we have some?'

"The boy, whose name was Hansel, nodded. So everyone stopped and picked and ate berries. When they were all filled up with berries, they went on their way again. Hansel and Gretal joined the others. So now there was quite a procession in the forest."

"What's a procession?" asked Russell.

"A parade," said Grandpa.

"Stop interrupting," said Teddy. "What happened next?"

"They went on until suddenly Snow White shouted, *'Stop.'*

" 'What is the matter?' asked Goldilocks, Little Red Riding Hood, Hansel and Gretel, and the little bear.

" 'I have no more M&M candies,' said Snow White. 'So I can't go any farther. If I do, I will get lost.'

" 'That's all right,' said the little bear, pointing straight ahead. 'Look over there.'

"Everyone looked where he was pointing. There was a big cave. And in the entrance to the cave sat a great big papa bear and a medium-size mama bear holding a tiny little baby bear. There were also three small bears, just the size of the bear that was lost. Only, of course, he wasn't lost anymore.

" 'Do come inside and have a treat,' said the medium-size mama bear.

" 'Is it porridge?' asked Goldilocks. 'I hate porridge, even when it is cooked just right.'

" 'Shhhh,' said Snow White. 'You will hurt the mama bear's feelings.'

" 'It's not porridge,' said the medium-size mama bear. 'I have bad luck whenever I make porridge. I have cookies and milk for all of you. So they all sat down inside the cave and ate cookies and drank milk. Even though they had just eaten all the black raspberries, they still had plenty of room. When they finished, Snow White, Goldilocks, and Hansel and Gretel were all very polite and thanked the mama bear for the lovely treat. Little Red Riding Hood couldn't speak to strangers, so she didn't say a word. But she smiled and gave her bouquet of flowers to the mama bear.

"Then it was time to say good-bye. The seven bears waved to the children. 'Come again,' they said.

"Snow White, Goldilocks, Little Red Riding Hood, and Hansel and Gretel all started home. Snow White followed the trail of M&Ms.

" 'Aren't you going to pick them up?' asked Hansel.

" 'No,' said Snow White. 'I'm not allowed to eat candy that has fallen on the ground. And, if they are still there tomorrow, the little bear will be able to find his way back to visit with us all again. Maybe he will even bring his little brother bears with him.'

" 'That would be fun,' said Gretel.

"Goldilocks agreed. Little Red Riding Hood thought so, too, but she couldn't say anything because she was not allowed to speak to strangers.

"Soon they came to the place where Hansel and Gretel had been picking berries. 'Good-bye,' they said. 'I hope we see you again.'

"Then they reached the spot where Little Red Riding Hood had been picking flowers. 'Good-bye,' she said. 'I had a lovely time.' "

"How come she was speaking? I thought she wasn't allowed to talk to strangers," said Nora.

"Well, by now they were all friends," said Grandpa. "And, of course, she could speak to her friends."

"Grandpa," said Teddy. "I didn't know that

13

Goldilocks and Little Red Riding Hood and Snow White and Hansel and Gretel were all friends."

"Of course they were," said Grandpa. "They all lived in the same forest, didn't they? It was different than living here in New York City, but it was the same, too. When children live near one another, they become good friends. Even if some are older and some are younger. Snow White was older than Little Red Riding Hood, but they were still friends. Just like you and Nora and Russell are not the same age, but you can still have fun together."

"That's right," said Nora.

"I told you there was a story about Snow White and the Seven Bears," said Russell proudly. "I was right."

Who's Who

Even though his parents had prepared him, even though Teddy and Nora had told him all about it, kindergarten was still full of surprises for Russell. He was going to school in a new building. He had a new teacher named Ms. Cassedy. And he stayed at school all day long.

Russell's mother bought him a lunch box to

take to school. He liked it very much. There were pictures of Mickey Mouse on the outside and a Thermos bottle inside. On the first day of school his lunch box was packed with things that Russell liked. There was a cream cheese and strawberry jam sandwich, a box of raisins, a banana, and two chocolate cookies. The Thermos was filled with milk.

Mrs. Michaels brought Russell to the door of the classroom. "This is Russell," she told Ms. Cassedy.

The teacher smiled at Russell. "Welcome to kindergarten," she said. Then she looked through a pile of yellow cardboard circles with green strings attached to them.

"Here is a necklace for you to wear," she told Russell.

He looked at the yellow disc. It read, RUS-SELL. He could recognize his name because of the two Ss in the middle and the two Ls at the end.

"Put it on," said Ms. Cassedy, handing it to him.

Russell didn't want to wear a necklace. Necklaces were for girls. But then he saw his old friend Jeremy standing nearby. Jeremy was wearing a necklace, so Russell decided that he would wear his, too.

"Bye, Russell," his mother said, bending down to give him a hug. "I'll be back to take you home when school is over." Then she walked out the door, and Russell was left with the new teacher and all of the other boys and girls. A whole day seemed like a long, long time.

Russell wasn't sure if he was going to like kindergarten as much as nursery school. He went over to Jeremy.

"Hi," he said. It was funny to see his old friend in this new classroom.

"Hi, R-u-s-s-e-l-l," Jeremy spelled out.

He looked down at his own necklace. It had different letters on it.

"Ms. Cassedy said we had to wear these so she would know who we are," he told Russell.

"That's silly," said Russell. "We already

know who we are. I'm Russell and you're Jeremy," he said. Then he had an idea. "Let's trade necklaces. Then we can pretend that I am Jeremy and you are Russell."

Jeremy laughed. That sounded like a good game to him.

"Don't tell anyone who you really are," said Russell. "And I won't tell anyone, either."

Ms. Cassedy called all the children to come and sit on the floor. "Whenever I blink the lights on and off," she said, "you must stop talking and stay where you are. That is one of the rules of our class." She walked over to the light switch and turned the lights on and off. "That is how I will do it when I want your attention."

Russell wondered if he could do that at home. If he turned the lights on and off, would his parents stop talking and pay attention to him?

Ms. Cassedy told the children the other rules of kindergarten. Most of the rules were like nursery school. No shouting. No running in the classroom. Taking turns. Sharing. There would be snack time every day. That was like nursery school, too. Russell hoped the snack was chocolate cookies.

Then Ms. Cassedy played the piano. She played songs that Russell already knew, such as, "There was a farmer had a dog and Bingo was his name-O." Jeremy sang very loud, and Ms. Cassedy said, "Good singing, Russell." That made Russell laugh. He and Jeremy were sure fooling the teacher.

Ms. Cassedy taught them a new song. They had to shake their right hand and then their left hand. Many of the boys and girls were not sure which was which. "Look," said Ms. Cassedy. "Here is an easy way to remember. If you hold your fingers together and your thumbs out, your left hand always makes an *L*." Russell had never noticed that before.

After the songs Ms. Cassedy took the children on a tour of the school building. They

19

went to the principal's office and they went to meet Mrs. Richards, the school nurse. They saw where the bathrooms were, and they even saw the first-grade classrooms. Russell saw Teddy. Even though Russell was pretending to be Jeremy, Teddy knew who he really was and waved to him. Russell waved back.

After the tour it was snack time. "Anna and Jeremy," said Ms. Cassedy, looking around the room and calling out two names from the yellow discs. "Today you can be my helpers." Jeremy was sitting next to Russell. He started to get up, but Russell pulled him back. "Don't forget. I'm Jeremy today and you are Russell."

Russell helped give out the cookies for snack time. He was so pleased with the job and with fooling Ms. Cassedy, he didn't even mind that they were having graham crackers and not chocolate cookies.

When snacks were over, everyone sat on the floor while Ms. Cassedy read a story. The day was passing quickly because there were so many things to do. Once Russell raised his hand to ask a question, and Ms. Cassedy called him Jeremy. Once the real Jeremy sneezed, and Ms. Cassedy said, "Bless you, Russell." and gave him a tissue to blow his nose. It was a very good game.

At lunchtime all the children took their lunch boxes from the cubbyholes where they had been stored. It was the first time that Russell drank milk from his new Thermos. His milk had stayed cold all morning, just like magic. His mother had told him that it would.

Jeremy was not eating much. "Don't you like your lunch?" asked Russell.

"I'm not hungry," said Jeremy.

"Can I have your apple?" said Russell. "Kindergarten makes me very hungry."

When the children finished eating, Ms. Cassedy took them outside to play in the schoolyard. "I'll race you to the fence," Russell said to Jeremy. Jeremy said he did not feel like running, so Russell ran by himself. He chased

two of the girls in his class. He had a good time running around. He was sorry when Ms. Cassedy clapped her hands and called everyone to come inside.

"There's no light switch outdoors," said Russell. "Wouldn't it be funny if she could turn the sun on and off?"

Jeremy didn't laugh. His face was flushed and he looked unhappy. "Are you okay?" Russell asked his friend.

Jeremy shook his head. "I don't feel good," he said.

When all the children were back in the classroom, Russell went over to Ms. Cassedy.

"He doesn't feel good," he said, pointing to Jeremy.

Ms. Cassedy went over to Jeremy and put her hand on his forehead. "I think you have a fever, Russell," she said. She told him she would call the school nurse. "She thinks I am you and you are me," the real Russell told Jeremy. He still thought it was a good joke, but Jeremy didn't care about games now.

Soon Mrs. Richards, the nurse, came into the room. "Come with me, Russell," she said to Jeremy. "We'll call your mother and tell her to come and take you home."

Jeremy followed Mrs. Richards. Mrs. Richards thought that Jeremy was named Russell, just like Ms. Cassedy did. They sure fooled everyone today.

Ms. Cassedy gave out sheets of paper and crayons. She told the children to make a picture of something they had done during the summer. The crayons were brand-new and had sharp points. It would be fun to draw with them. But just as Russell began drawing, he thought of something. If Mrs. Richards and Ms. Cassedy thought that it was Russell who was sick, they would not call Jeremy's mother. Russell's mother would come to take Jeremy home.

Russell put the crayon down on the table and stood up. He walked over to Ms. Cassedy.

"What's the matter, Jeremy?" she asked. "Can't you think of anything to draw?"

"I'm Russell," said Russell.

Ms. Cassedy smiled and put her arm around him. "Do you want to go home early like Russell?" she asked. "Russell is not feeling well. It will be time for the rest of us to go home before you know it, Jeremy."

"I'm not Jeremy," said Russell. "I'm Russell."

"J-e-r-e-m-y spells Jeremy," said the teacher, pointing to the letters on the necklace that he was wearing.

"I know," said Russell. "And R-u-s-s-e-l-l spells Russell. "That's who I am. Russell."

"How did you get the wrong necklace?" asked Ms. Cassedy, looking confused.

"I traded with Jeremy this morning," said Russell. "It was a game. Today I was Jeremy, and Jeremy was Russell. But I'm not sick and you should tell Mrs. Richards. She said she was going to call my mother."

Ms. Cassedy went to the telephone and

called the nurse. When she finished, she turned to Russell. "Soon I will know who's who in this class," she said. "But until I do, everyone must wear the right necklace. Do you understand?"

"Yes," said Russell.

"Good," said Ms. Cassedy, smiling at him. "I certainly won't forget who you are tomorrow!"

She went to the light switch and turned the lights on and off. "Finish up your pictures," she told the children when they all looked up at her.

Russell sat down at the table and quickly colored in the green grass in his picture. It had been fun pretending to be Jeremy, he thought. But he was glad to be the real Russell again. He was glad that he wasn't sick like Jeremy. He hoped Jeremy would get better real fast. On the top of his paper he wrote his own name with the two *S*s in the middle and the two *L*s at the end. When his mother came to take him home, he would show her how he had learned to make an *L* with his left hand.

Kindergarten was fun. He would be glad to come back again tomorrow and be Russell all day long.

Bath Time

Every evening, winter or summer, spring or fall, Russell took a bath before he went to bed. And every evening, winter or summer, spring or fall, he complained. It wasn't that he didn't like baths. He knew that once he had taken his bath, it was time to go to bed. It was much more fun to stay awake and play. Sleep was so boring.

Over the years Russell had accumulated a whole box of bathtub toys. He had a rubber frog, two rubber fish, and a rubber duck, and they all floated in the water. He also had a whole fleet of boats and some plastic dolls that he pretended were sailors. His mother put bubble-bath powder into the water so he could play with the soap bubbles and cover his body with the white foam. He could make himself a beard of bubbles and even a mustache (but the mustache usually made him sneeze).

Elisa always had her bath first. Because she was so little, Russell's mother had to wash her and watch over her each minute that she was in the bathtub. Elisa splashed and laughed in the water. She liked her baths, and she didn't seem to mind that when bath time was over it was bedtime. Once Elisa was tucked into her crib, it was time for Russell to take his bath.

"Can't I wait a little longer?" he always asked.

"If you come right now, you'll have more

time to play in the water," his mother told him.

"I don't want to play in the water," Russell said. "I want to play with my cars. Cars don't go in the water."

"But boys do," said his mother, taking him by the arm. "Come on now. March."

Russell marched into the bathroom. His mother adjusted the temperature of the water and began to fill the tub. "It's too early to take my bath," Russell protested, but he took off his sneakers and his socks. He took off his shorts. Then he pulled the box of toys from under the tub and threw each toy into the water. He liked the splashes that they made.

"Come on," said his mother, helping him remove his T-shirt. "Stop dawdling."

Russell climbed out of his underpants and lifted a foot over the edge of the tub. He stuck his big toe into the water. "It's too hot," he said.

Mrs. Michaels ran a little more cold water into the tub and poured the bubble-bath powder in, too. Russell put his second foot into the water and sat down. He began swishing the bubbles around so they would get bigger and bigger. "I'll call you in twenty minutes," said Mrs. Michaels, handing Russell the washcloth. "Don't forget to wash yourself, too."

Russell took the washcloth and pretended to wash himself for a minute while his mother was still in the bathroom. As soon as she left he dropped it into the water. He never bothered using it when he was alone. He knew that he got perfectly clean just by sitting in the warm, soapy water.

Mrs. Michaels went out of the bathroom, closing the door partway so there wouldn't be a draft. She always left it open a bit so Russell could call her. Sometimes he got soap in his eyes and she would come and give him a towel so he could rub them until they felt better.

Russell took his boats and put them in a line. Then he took the frog and dropped him down on top of the boats. The boats sank, but because they were plastic, they righted themselves again quickly. From the bathtub Russell could hear the telephone ringing. He heard his mother answer it. He wondered who she was speaking to, but as the fish floated up between his legs, he forgot about his mother and the telephone and made a storm at sea. He splashed the water around in the tub, and the boats and the frog and the fish and the duck sank under the waves. When they popped up from the sudsy water, he splashed them under again. The water was just the right temperature, and he wished he could play forever and ever and not have to go to bed.

Russell took his washcloth. He plopped the wet cloth down on top of the frog. The frog sank to the bottom of the tub and couldn't float up with the cloth weighing it down. That was fun. Russell tried plopping the cloth on each of the boats and on the fish and the duck, too. He took the little plastic people and taught them how to swim in the water. His father had promised to teach Russell how to swim when he was older. Russell pretended he

was swimming in the bathtub. He leaned back and tried to float in the water. The back of his hair got wet, but he didn't care. Sometimes, when he didn't have soap bubbles in the water, he put his face in and blew bubbles himself. Nora said that was the way the children learned to swim at the day camp she went to.

Nora and Teddy both knew how to swim. Russell would learn someday, too. Right now, pretending to swim in the bath was good enough. On hot days Nora and Teddy and Russell put on their bathing suits and played in the sprinkler at the wading pool in the park. Eugene Spencer, who also lived in their building, said that he was too old to do that. Elisa was too little. Someone might knock her over. Russell was glad that he was just the right age for the sprinkler.

Russell heard his mother hang up the phone and say something to his father. Then he heard the television. His parents must be watching a program. He yawned and examined the plastic people. "You need a good wash," he told them. Using the washcloth he carefully scrubbed each one. "Look at these knees," he said, the way his mother sometimes said to him.

The plastic lady slipped out of Russell's hand and fell into the water. "Don't worry," he called to her. "Big Russell will rescue you!" He plunged his hand into the water and caught the toy. "I am big and strong," Russell boasted to the plastic lady. He let her slip out of his fingers again so that he could rescue her a second time.

Then Big Russell splashed around in the water. He was able to make the splashes go over the top of the tub and onto the floor. He knew his mother didn't like him to get the floor all wet, but sometimes when he was playing Big Russell, he just couldn't help it.

It was fun playing in the water, he thought. Fish were lucky to stay in water all the time. They never went to bed, he thought as he yawned again. Dogs and cats went to sleep like people. But fish kept swimming around and around.

He never saw a fish with its eyes closed. Even in the market when his mother bought fish for dinner, the fish eyes were open. Russell wondered if he could keep his eyes open under the water. Eugene Spencer said that you needed to do that if you wanted to be a good swimmer. There was too much soap in the water now. Tomorrow night, if he remembered, Russell would try to keep his eyes open under the water.

He looked at his fingers. They were all wrinkled like raisins, except they were pink and not the color of raisins. Sometimes his mother bought white raisins. White raisins really were yellow. Russell's fingers looked like raisins, but they weren't white and they weren't yellow. He tasted his finger. It tasted soapy. It didn't taste like a raisin at all.

He yawned again. He wondered when it would be bedtime. He wondered if fish got wrinkled from the water. He had never seen a wrinkled fish. Maybe they were wrinkled underneath their scales. He wondered what it felt like to have scales. Maybe if he had scales, he wouldn't get wrinkled when he took his bath.

He yawned and almost rubbed his eyes. Luckily he remembered that his hands were soapy. He didn't want to get soap in his eyes. It made them tear. He wondered if fish could cry. No one would know if they did because the tears would go into the water. Tears were salty. Maybe the reason the ocean was salty was because fish had cried in the water. He would have to remember to ask his father.

"I'll call Ginny in the morning," Mrs. Michaels said as she walked toward the bathroom door. "I'll ask if she and Alex want to go to the concert with us."

The bathroom door opened. "My goodness!" said Mrs. Michaels. "What are you doing here?"

Russell looked at his mother standing in the doorway. Mothers could be so silly. "I'm taking my bath," he reminded her.

"Your bath? It's ten o'clock at night."

"Ten o'clock?" asked Russell. He couldn't tell time, but he knew that ten o'clock was way past his bedtime. He went to sleep at the number eight.

"Why didn't you call me?" she asked.

"I never call you when I take a bath unless I get soap in my eyes," Russell said. "I didn't get any soap in my eyes tonight."

"Oh, Russell, I forgot all about you!" said Mrs. Michaels.

"What did you do?" asked Russell's father, coming into the bathroom. "Russell, what are you doing in here?" he asked.

Fathers could be silly, too, Russell thought. "I'm taking my bath," he said.

"It was getting that long-distance phone call from my friend Caroline. I lost all track of time and I forgot that I hadn't put you to bed."

"It's okay," said Russell, yawning. "I was busy playing. And getting washed, too," he added quickly.

Mrs. Michaels put her hand in the water. "It's like ice,"she said. "I'm so sorry, Russell."

She helped him out of the tub and rubbed him with the big fluffy bath towel. Inside the tub Russell hadn't felt cold at all. But now that he was out, he began to shiver.

"I'm raisins all over," he said to his parents, and held out his wrinkled hands.

"Delicious," said his mother, kissing his fingers.

"Could I turn into a real raisin?" Russell asked.

"Of course not," said his father.

"Could I turn into a fish?"

"Never," said his mother. "But you know what you did turn into?"

"What?" asked Russell.

"You turned into the cleanest boy in New York City."

"He's turned into the cleanest boy in the

whole world," said Mr. Michaels. He helped Russell put on his pajamas. And then both his parents tucked him into bed, the cleanest boy in the world who had taken the longest bath in the world.

Playing with Elisa

Elisa was silly. Even though she had lots of toys, her favorite game was playing with the five-pound bag of potatoes in the cupboard. Russell's mother bought the potatoes to cook for supper. Sometimes she made baked potatoes, sometimes she made mashed potatoes, and sometimes she made home fries. But Elisa thought potatoes were toys. As long as she didn't take them out of the kitchen, Mrs. Michaels let her play with them. She piled the potatoes into towers, she counted with them, and she rolled them on the floor as if they were rubber balls. Because potatoes grow underneath the earth, they were always dusty. Elisa got very dirty playing with potatoes.

Now that she was two years old, Elisa went to a play group two mornings a week, and she had friends who came to play with her.

"Elisa is too little to have friends," Russell said when he heard that a boy named Ian was coming to visit his sister. Elisa was just a baby.

"You had friends when you were her age," his mother reminded him. "When you were two years old, Teddy was three and Nora was five, and you all played together."

Russell couldn't remember Nora being the same age that he was now. And he didn't believe that Nora would have played with him if he was as bad at games as Elisa.

Ian and Elisa chased each other around the

apartment and laughed. They thought that was a game. They built towers with blocks, but they liked knocking them down more than they liked building them. They colored with crayons, but all they did was make squiggly lines on the paper. They didn't know how to draw pictures. Russell didn't want to play with them. He was glad to be off at his friend Jeremy's house when Ian came over. Russell was sure that he had not been so babyish when he was two years old.

One Saturday a new friend of Elisa's came to visit. Her name was Cissie Henderson. Cissie was big. She was almost as big as Russell.

"Are you sure she is two years old?" he asked his mother.

"Yes. She was born the same week as Elisa," said Mrs. Michaels.

"Then why is she so big?" asked Russell.

"Both her parents are tall," his mother explained. "She's going to grow into a very tall girl."

Russell was sure that Cissie was four or even

five years old. She looked like she could be in his kindergarten class. But as he watched her running around after Elisa, he could tell that she was just a baby after all. That Saturday Russell didn't have a play date with any of his friends so he had to be around.

Cissie sat down to lunch with Russell and Elisa. Mrs. Michaels had made grilled cheese sandwiches and cut them into squares so that each child would have four little sandwiches. She called them postage stamps. They were good to eat that way, even though Russell had never seen a letter with a stamp as big as one of those little square sandwiches. There was also apple juice to drink and chocolate pudding for dessert. Russell ate one, and then a second, postage stamp. Elisa was still eating her first one. Cissie ate fast. She took a sandwich in each hand and gobbled them up. She just pushed the whole sandwich into her mouth. Then she grabbed two more. They disappeared as quickly as the first two. Russell stopped eating and watched with amazement.

No wonder Cissie was so big, he thought. She ate all the sandwiches left on the serving plate. She drained the juice from the glass and called out for more. "More juice. More juice," she shouted to Mrs. Michaels, who was standing at the sink with her back to the children.

"You should say please," Russell told her. His mother would have scolded him if he had shouted that way. But she just smiled at Cissie and poured more apple juice into her glass.

Each child was given a dish of pudding. There was no way big Cissie could eat more than her share now, Russell thought. But he was wrong. As soon as she had scraped all the pudding from her own dish, Cissie reached over and stuck her spoon into Elisa's. Elisa liked having her friend eat from the same dish. She thought it was a good joke and didn't protest at all. In a flash all the pudding in Elisa's dish was gone, too. Then Cissie turned toward Russell.

"Hey, you can't have my pudding," he said, covering the dish with his hands.

Cissie hit Russell with her spoon. "Stop that!" cried Russell. He rubbed his hand where Cissie had hit him. As soon as his hand was off the pudding dish, Cissie stuck her spoon inside it. She scooped up a big spoonful of the pudding and put it into her mouth.

"Stop that, you big pig!" Russell shouted, giving her a shove.

"Pig. Pig." Elisa laughed.

Mrs. Michaels had been making a phone call. Now she came running as Cissie began to howl. "Did you hit Cissie?" she demanded.

"I just pushed her away from my pudding," said Russell.

"Cissie is Elisa's guest, and she is only a little girl," his mother scolded. "You are a big boy and you know that you have to be gentle with her. You must treat her just as nicely as you would treat any of your own friends."

"It isn't fair," Russell shouted. "My friends don't steal my pudding." He got up from the table. He hoped that Cissie would go home soon.

Mrs. Michaels began clearing the dishes, and the two girls ran into the bedroom. Russell and Elisa shared the same bedroom, so Russell decided that he would stay in the living room. Cissie and Elisa ran after him. Russell went into the kitchen. "Cissie and Elisa are following me," he complained.

"They want to play with you," said his mother.

"Well, I don't want to play with them."

"There must be some game you could all play together," said Mrs. Michaels. "How about hide-and-seek?"

Hide-and-seek was one of the few games that Russell could play with his sister. It was always easy to find Elisa. She thought that if she covered her eyes, no one could see her. But Russell played with her, anyway. He liked to hide behind the big armchair in the living room and jump out and scare her.

"Okay," said Russell now. He had nothing else to do.

"I hide. I hide," Elisa shouted.

"Cissie, you and Elisa go and hide, and Russell will come looking for you," said Mrs. Michaels.

Russell put his hands over his eyes and counted slowly to twenty-five. "Ready or not, here I come," he called.

He could hear the two girls giggling behind the sofa. But even though he knew where they were, he walked in the opposite direction. He pretended to look for them in the kitchen. "Not here," he said, looking under the kitchen table. He went all over the apartment. "Not here," he said, looking behind the armchair in the living room.

Slowly he approached the sofa. Instead of looking behind it he sat down. "I don't know where they are," he said. That was part of the game. Elisa came jumping out and shouted. "I foolded you. I foolded you."

"I foolded you. I foolded you," shouted Cissie.

Then it was Russell's turn to fool the girls.

"Close your eyes while I hide," he told them.

The girls got down on their knees and rested their heads on the sofa cushions. They covered their eyes. "One-two-seven-four ..." Elisa counted. That was the way she counted potatoes, too. She knew all the numbers, but she didn't know them in order.

Russell considered all his usual hiding places: the armchair, behind the bathroom door, the hall closet. He decided to hide in the closet in his parents' bedroom. He had never hidden there before, and it would take the girls a long time to find him. Squatting down in the closet next to his mother's shoes, he heard the girls racing through the apartment looking for him. It was good to have a little time to himself, but after a minute or two, he began to wonder if they were ever going to come. This hiding place is too hard to guess, Russell decided. He crept out of the closet and tiptoed toward the bathroom. Just as he got behind the door, he heard the girls entering his parents' bedroom.

"Not here," said Elisa.

"Not here," echoed Cissie.

Russell waited, smiling to himself. He heard them approaching the bathroom. In a moment he would jump out at them.

"Let's look in the kitchen," said Cissie. The girls turned around and went in the direction of the kitchen. Russell couldn't jump out at them if they weren't nearby.

He crept out of the bathroom and walked quietly toward the kitchen. He hid behind the armchair in the living room and waited. The girls were still in the kitchen.

He crept out from behind the chair. From the kitchen doorway he could see that they were sitting at the table. Why weren't they looking for him? He wasn't in the kitchen. Even a two-year-old could figure that out.

He saw his mother give the girls sheets of paper. "Try not to spill the water," she said. They were painting with Elisa's watercolors. Russell was angry.

He marched into the kitchen. "You're supposed to be looking for me," he demanded.

"No more hide-and-seek," said Elisa. "We're painting."

"You can't stop a game in the middle like that," Russell protested. "It's not fair."

"Russell," Mrs. Michaels reminded her son. "They're much littler than you. They don't always understand about the rules of the game. I'll keep them busy in here if you want to play in your room."

"Good," said Russell, marching off. "I don't want to play with them anymore."

He went to his bedroom. He was glad that he didn't have to play with those babies. They didn't even know how to play, anyhow. He looked at his cars, but he didn't feel like playing with them. He looked at his Lego set, but he didn't feel like playing with that, either. He looked at his books and his puzzles. Nothing appealed to him.

Russell sat on his bed and wondered what to do. He wished he could have gone to Jeremy's house, but Jeremy had a sore throat. He wished he could have gone to play with Nora and Teddy, but they had gone to visit their cousins. There was nothing to do.

Russell got up off his bed and went into the kitchen. He just wanted to see what Elisa and Cissie were doing now. He really didn't want to play with them. The girls had stopped painting.

"What are you doing?" Russell asked Elisa.

"Nothing," said Elisa.

"Nothing," said Cissie.

"What are you going to do?" asked Russell.

"I don't know," said Elisa.

"I don't know," said Cissie.

"I know," said Russell. "Potatoes!"

"Potatoes!" Cissie shrieked happily.

Russell started to laugh. Poor Cissie thought she was going to get some potatoes to eat. Wouldn't she be surprised that potatoes was a game?

Elisa opened the cupboard where the potatoes were stored and pulled them out. Russell sat down on the floor with the girls. It was good that he remembered how much Elisa liked playing with potatoes, he thought.

"Look," said Russell, lining up the potatoes. "I am going to teach you how to count."

"I count," said Elisa.

"I count," said Cissie.

"Sure you count," said Russell. "But you count all wrong. You count the baby way. I'm going to teach you how big boys and girls count in kindergarten."

He lined up the potatoes in a neat row. "One, two, three . . ." he began. Counting potatoes on the kitchen floor was baby stuff, he thought. Still, the least he could do was play with his sister and her friend. After all, Teddy and Nora had played with him when he was two years old. That was how he learned to be such a smart big boy. Elisa was lucky to have him to teach her. And Cissie was lucky, too. "One, two, three, four . . ."

The Birthday Monster

"I've been waiting for my birthday for a hundred years," Russell said.

"Well, you won't have to wait much longer," said his mother. "Tomorrow is *the* day."

Russell smiled happily. Tomorrow he would be six years old. He was going to have a birthday party with eight guests, and it was going to be the best birthday party ever.

At first his parents had said that there could only be six children at the party because he would be six years old. But then they started making the list. Russell was going to invite Teddy, who lived right in the same building and had been his friend since he was a baby. He would invite Teddy's sister Nora, and he would invite Eugene Spencer, who was the only other child who lived in the apartment building (not counting Elisa). Of course, Elisa was coming to the party! So that made four guests, and Russell still had to have his friends from school. He had to invite Jeremy. Russell had gone to his birthday party just two weeks ago. And he had to invite Peter and Daniel, who were in his kindergarten class, too. That made seven guests.

"Well, we have to invite your cousin Howie. He is practically the same age as you," said Mrs. Michaels. "That makes eight."

Eight guests meant eight presents. Russell liked that. He had the whole party planned in his head. When he went to Jeremy's party, all the children had gone outside to the park and played hide-and-seek and tag and swung on the swings before they went back to the house for ice cream and cake. That was what Russell wanted to do at his party, too.

But when he looked out of the window the morning of his birthday, he could see that it was raining. Even though it was his birthday, Russell felt grumpy. Why did it always rain when he wanted the sun to be shining? It wasn't fair!

Just then his father came into the room, and Russell cheered up. "This was too big to wrap," said Mr. Michaels. He was pushing a two-wheel bike into Russell's bedroom.

"Is that for me?" asked Russell. The bike was big and red and just like the one that Teddy had.

"Of course it's for you," said his father,

smiling. "I'm going to teach you how to ride it."

Russell climbed up on the bike while his father supported him so it wouldn't tip over. He could imagine himself riding fast through the park with all the other big kids. No more riding a baby tricycle for him. After all, now he was six years old.

"Look," said Mr. Michaels. "Here is a horn to warn people to keep out of your way."

Russell squeezed the rubber ball at the end of the horn. It made a wonderful sound.

"I wish I could go riding right now," he said.

"It's raining," Mr. Michaels reminded him. "We'll have plenty of other chances."

Russell felt gloomy again. He had forgotten about the rain.

"Come," called his mother, who had been standing nearby with Elisa. "There are other presents waiting for the birthday boy in the kitchen."

On the kitchen table, next to the breakfast dishes, Russell found his other gifts. He ripped the paper off them quickly. He had waited so long for all these presents. There was a blue car that ran on a battery in the first package. When you turned it on, it could go all across the room by itself and then turn around and come back again. Jeremy had gotten a car just like it for his birthday, except Jeremy's car was red. Russell wished his car was red like his new bike. Red was his favorite color.

In the next package he found a chalkboard and chalk.

"I can hang the chalkboard up on the wall of your room," said his father.

"Will you do it right away?" asked Russell. He saw that there was an eraser in the package, too.

"As soon as I have my coffee," his father promised.

The next package held a red wool sweater and a matching hat that his grandmother had made for Russell. Even though it was red, Russell was disappointed. He didn't want clothes for a birthday present. He only wanted toys.

"Grandma worked on that a long time," said his mother. "Look, she even stitched your initials on it." She pointed to the *RM* for Russell Michaels. It was on both the sweater and the hat. "You can wear it when you ride your new bike."

Russell sighed. He remembered that it was raining so he couldn't ride his new bike.

There was only one package left. It was very small, and when Russell shook it, it made a squishy sound. He couldn't imagine what it could be.

"That gift is from Elisa," said his mother. How could that be? Elisa didn't have any money, and she couldn't go into a store and buy a present. Russell quickly ripped the paper off the gift. It was a bottle of bubbles and a little wand.

"This is a baby present," said Russell,

throwing it down on the table. "This isn't a good present for a boy six years old."

"When you spilled your bottle of bubbles in the park last week, you cried because you couldn't make any more," Mrs. Michaels reminded him. "Elisa thought you would like a new bottle."

"Last week I was only five years old," said Russell. "Now I am six!" There was nothing more to open. Russell sighed. "What time will my friends come?" he asked.

Russell's guests came at two o'clock. By that time, his father had fastened the chalkboard to the wall and Russell had written on it with white, pink, and yellow chalk and erased his letters with the eraser many times. He had also sat on his new bike and played with his new blue car, running it back and forth in every room of the apartment. At lunchtime Russell ate very little. He was too excited thinking about the party, and besides, he wanted to have plenty of room for the ice cream and cake. He hadn't seen the cake, but he had seen one just like it in the bakery window and he had pointed it out to his mother. It was shaped like a car. "That's the cake that I want for my birthday," he had told her, and she had promised him that he would have one just like it. Now he was sorry that he hadn't asked for a cake shaped like a two-wheeler.

Promptly at two o'clock the door bell rang and the guests began to arrive. Nora and Teddy came first. Russell was glad to see them but was disappointed that they had brought only one gift between them.

"Now I'm the same as you," he reminded Teddy. They were both six years old now.

He took the package from Nora and put it on the table in the living room. He would have to wait until later to open all his presents together.

The door bell rang again. It was Jeremy. He carried a big package. Russell grabbed it and gave it a shake. He could hear that there were pieces inside.

The next time the door bell rang, it was Eugene Spencer and cousin Howie with Aunt Jean. They were standing together even though Howie and Eugene Spencer had never met before. A moment later Peter and Daniel arrived, too. The pile of gifts on the table was getting very high. "Can't I open them now?" Russell begged.

"Not yet," said his mother. "Later, when it's time for the birthday cake."

It made Russell angry to have to wait, but then he remembered his new bicycle in the bedroom. "Come see what I got already!" he shouted, and he led the way toward his room.

"It's just like mine," said Teddy. "We can ride together."

"First you have to learn how to ride it," Nora reminded Russell.

"Hey. You can't write on that," Russell said to Teddy. He was in the middle of writing his name on the new chalkboard.

"Why not?" Teddy asked.

"I didn't say you could," said Russell.

Teddy didn't say anything, but Nora said, "How come you are acting so mean, Russell? Just because it's your birthday you think you're a big shot."

Mrs. Michaels came into the bedroom. She was holding Elisa's hand. Russell's sister was wearing a pink party dress and had pink ribbons in her hair.

"Come," Mrs. Michaels called to the children. "We are going to play a game of hot potato."

"Good," said Jeremy. "I like that game."

"Give me the potato first," Russell demanded when all the children except Elisa were sitting in a circle on the living room floor.

"You may go first because you are the birthday boy," said his mother. She handed the potato to Russell, and then she turned on the phonograph. While the music played the children passed the potato around and around in the circle. When the music stopped, whoever had the potato in their hand would be out of the game. Russell had played this at other parties, too. Sometimes they used a ball or an orange, but they always called it hot potato. He was glad that at his party they were using a real potato.

The music stopped, and Howie was out.

The music began again. Peter and then Daniel were out. Then Eugene Spencer was out. The next person holding the potato when the music stopped was Jeremy. Then Nora was out. Only Teddy and Russell were left. "I bet I win," said Russell. "It's my birthday!"

"No way," said Nora. "Teddy's faster than you."

Russell and Teddy tossed the potato back and forth. Then the music stopped. "I win. I win," Russell shouted, because Teddy was holding the potato. "What's my prize?" At Jeremy's party the winner of the hot potato game had gotten a big box of crayons.

"You win the potato," said Mrs. Michaels. "I will bake it for your supper."

"A potato isn't a prize!" Russell protested. "It's stupid. I don't want a potato for a prize." He threw it down on the floor and stamped his foot.

"Russell," said his mother in a firm voice, "you are not being a good sport."

All of the children sat quietly and looked at Russell. He had made a fuss, but you shouldn't be scolded on your birthday!

"When is Russell going to open his presents?" Nora asked.

"Can I open them now?" asked Russell.

"What a good idea," said Mrs. Michaels.

Russell rushed over to the table where his gifts were waiting. He tore the paper off the top present. Inside was a T-shirt with his name on it. "That's from me," called Peter, but Russell was already opening the next box. He got a game of Chinese checkers. There was a new paint set in the package underneath that. The next box was a big one. It was a board game.

He wished the box had been full of little cars.

"That one's from me," Jeremy called out as Russell began tearing the paper off still another gift. It was another board game, just like the other one that he had received a moment before.

He threw it on the floor. "I don't want another one. I didn't even want the first one."

"Russell," his father said sternly. "Say thank you to all your friends."

"Birthdays turn them into monsters," said Aunt Jean.

"I'm not a monster!" said Russell. He didn't want to say thank you. It was his birthday. He shouldn't have to say or do anything he didn't want to on his birthday.

"You still didn't open the present we gave you," Teddy pointed out. Nora and Teddy had arrived first, so their gift was at the bottom of the pile. Now it was half-hidden by all the torn wrapping paper and ribbons.

Russell snatched the package and tore the paper off. It was a book.

"I can't read," he said when he saw what his friends had given him.

"Ask your mother and father to read it to you," said Teddy. "That's what mine do."

"Of course," said Mrs. Michaels. "It will be a wonderful book for reading tonight at bedtime."

Russell looked through the wrapping paper. There were no more presents.

"You should have given me two presents," he said, turning to Nora and Teddy. "It isn't fair that you gave me only one present from both of you."

Nora stamped her foot. "You're just plain mean today," she said.

"I don't like this party," Teddy said. "I want to go home."

"You made Teddy feel bad," said Nora. "It's all your fault, Russell."

Russell felt awful. He had waited so long for this day, and everything seemed to have gone wrong. It was raining and he didn't think that was fair. And the presents he had gotten didn't seem as good as the presents he watched other children open at their birthday parties. And now, worst of all, Teddy wanted to go home from his party.

"Please don't go, Teddy," Russell said. "I'm sorry that I made you feel bad." He picked up the book Teddy and Nora had given him. "This is a very nice book. Thank you."

Teddy still didn't say anything.

"You could sit next to me and have the first piece of cake," Russell offered.

"Let's all sit down and have cake," said Mrs. Michaels. "This cake is from the new French bakery on Broadway," she said as she brought it to the table.

"My teacher taught us how to count up to ten in French," said Eugene Spencer.

"I speak English," said Teddy. He sat down next to Russell and smiled at his friend.

"My father can speak Hebrew," said Daniel.

"Mrs. Rodriguez on the second floor speaks Spanish," said Nora.

Mount Lebanon Academy
P.O. Box 10357
Pittsburgh, PA 15234

"I speak Spinach," said Russell.

"How can you speak Spinach? It's a food," said Howie, making a face.

"It sounds like this," said Russell. "Foomy, quish bun bun." He looked at his friends. "Kwalpy dolpy jung."

"Mush push zanko pooh," said Nora. She had learned the new language quickly.

"Booey grondo wiss," said Teddy.

Soon all of the children were speaking Spinach.

They sat around the table and sang "Happy Birthday" to Russell.

"Now sing it in Spinach," he said.

Everyone had their own version, but the melody was the same, and it sounded a bit like "Gooky smooky a boo, gooky smooky a boo."

There were two kinds of ice cream, chocolate and vanilla. "In Spinach it's smoocolate and panilla," said Russell.

It didn't matter what it was called, the ice cream and the cake shaped like a car were delicious, and everyone had second helpings of everything.

Everyone was laughing when it was time to go home.

"This was a good party, after all," Teddy told Russell. "You can come to my party next month, too."

Mrs. Michaels gave everyone a party bag filled with candies and a surprise. Nora opened her bag to peek inside. "Bubbles!" she called out happily. No one seemed to think that bubbles were babyish.

Russell went to his bedroom and found his little bottle of bubbles. It was on his chest of drawers with his new games and his new red sweater and hat. He sat on the living room floor and opened the bottle. He saw his mother watching him. He was waiting for her to tell him not to spill the bubbles on the rug. But she didn't. Now that he was six years old, he was already more careful.

Russell dipped the wand into the bubble liquid and blew gently. Many, many bubbles blew into the air. Elisa came running and tried to catch them. Russell made more and more bubbles. It was fun.

The bubbles broke when Elisa touched them, but it didn't matter. Russell could make as many as he wanted.

"Ubbli ubbli ooo," said Elisa.

"Don't talk baby talk," said Mr. Michaels. "You know those are bubbles, Elisa."

"She's speaking Spinach," Russell told his parents. "It means she wishes she was six years old and had a happy birthday today like I did."

"Ubbi ubbli ooo," said Elisa again.

Wheels

First there was rain, then a late snow, and then rain again. So it was three weeks between the time that Russell got his new birthday bicycle and the first day that he took it outdoors to ride.

Russell was very proud of his bike. He liked the bright red color, and he liked the horn that made such a loud honking sound whenever he squeezed the rubber end of it. Best of all, he liked having two big wheels instead of three. Bikes with three wheels were for babies.

The first sunny Saturday in April was perfect for riding his bicycle. Russell's father took him outside to teach him how. Riding on two wheels looked so easy when Nora and Teddy and Eugene Spencer did it. But when Russell tried to roll along on just two wheels, somehow the bike kept tipping over. Mr. Michaels held the bike up with both hands. "Don't worry. I won't let you fall," he promised.

Russell felt scared, but he didn't want anyone to know. He tried again. It was hard work pushing the pedals.

"I need a rest," he told his father.

"Good idea," said Mr. Michaels. "I forgot how hard it is to learn to ride a two-wheeler."

"Did you ever teach anyone before?" asked Russell.

"I taught Aunt Jean when she was a little girl."

Russell tried to imagine his aunt riding a

bike. He tried to imagine her being a little girl. He couldn't imagine either.

"Are you sure you taught her?" he asked. He had never seen his aunt riding a bike.

"Of course, I'm sure. Ask her yourself the next time you see her," said Mr. Michaels.

"Who taught you?" Russell asked. Talking with his father about when he was small was fun. It was more fun than trying to ride the bike.

"That's a good question," said Mr. Michaels. "I can't remember. It seems as if I've always known how to ride."

"I wish I was born knowing," said Russell as his father picked up the bicycle that had been leaning against the building's stoop.

"Come. Let's try again," he said.

They tried again. And again. And again. Russell was feeling hotter and hotter.

"I want to take off my jacket," he said. "I'll ride better without it."

"There's a sharp breeze," said Mr. Michaels. "You don't want to catch cold."

"I won't catch cold," Russell promised, but his father still wouldn't let him take off his jacket.

"Hi, there. How's it going?" called out Mrs. Resnick.

Russell didn't answer. "Where are Teddy and Nora?" he asked instead.

"They're spending the day with their grand-parents. I'll tell them I saw you riding your two-wheeler," Mrs. Resnick said, and went on her way.

"Russell isn't old enough to ride that big bike," said the nosey neighbor that the children all called Mrs. Mind-Your-Own-Business. Today was one day when Russell sure wished she would. He was beginning to worry that she was right. Maybe he was too young to ride a two-wheel bike. But then he reminded himself that Teddy was six years old and he could ride. That meant that Russell was big enough, too.

As soon as their neighbor left, Russell said, "I had enough practice."

"You know, you have to practice a lot to

learn how to ride a bike," said his father.

"I'll practice some more tomorrow," Russell promised. "Unless it rains," he added. He hoped it would. If he couldn't practice because of the weather, then it wasn't his fault.

It did not rain the next day. "Come," Mr. Michaels called to him. "Let's give the bike another try."

Russell didn't want to give the bike another try, but he didn't tell his father that. Slowly he put his jacket on and followed his father into the elevator. His father pushed the bicycle.

Mrs. Wurmbrand and her daughter were in the elevator when they got in. "Russell, is this big bike yours?" she asked.

Russell nodded his head.

"You certainly are growing up," she said, smiling at him.

That made Russell feel better. He *was* growing up. And today he bet he would be able to ride the bike.

But, out on the street, with his father pushing the bike and Russell straining to keep his

feet on the pedals, he didn't feel so grown-up after all. How come everyone else could learn how to ride a bike and he couldn't?

"I want to go upstairs," said Russell. "I don't want to ride this old bike."

"You haven't given it much of a chance," his father pointed out. "It takes more effort to learn to ride than you thought. But that doesn't mean you should give up so soon."

"I don't want to ride," said Russell, stamping his foot. "I don't like two-wheel bicycles anyhow."

"All right," said Mr. Michaels. "Let's call it a day. We can try again another time when you feel more like it. I remember I had a hard time learning how to ride when I was your age."

"Back again so soon?" asked Henry, the doorman. Russell didn't say a word.

The next day when Russell went to the park, he took his old tricycle. "Are you still riding that?" asked Nora. "Why aren't you riding your new bike?"

"I like my tricycle," said Russell.

"You're too big for a tricycle," said Eugene Spencer, riding by on his two-wheel bike.

The next day Russell didn't take any bike to the park. That evening Russell's father brought home a package. "I think this may help you," he told his son as he took a bar with a pair of small wheels out of the package. He fastened them onto the back of Russell's birthday bicycle.

"These are training wheels," Mr. Michaels explained. "They'll help you balance. After a while I'll raise them, and they'll give you just a little support. Then I'll take them off altogether and you'll be riding. You'll be teaching yourself."

It sounded like a good way to learn.

"Training wheels!" said Nora. "You don't need training wheels. I learned to ride without them. And so did Teddy. Now you have four wheels on your bike like a baby."

"I'm not a baby," Russell protested. "I'm six years old, just like Teddy."

81

"I'm practically seven," Teddy reminded him.

Russell ignored that and rode off on his bicycle. He pretended the training wheels weren't there. He was riding along on his big new bike like the other big kids. He rode standing up, the way the big kids did, and he waved his hand to his mother as he passed the bench where she was sitting. He had always liked the way the big kids could ride their bikes using just one hand.

After that, every sunny afternoon Russell asked his mother to take him to the park. He didn't want to go anywhere else, not to the zoo, not to visit his cousin Howie, not to the library. One evening his father adjusted the little training wheels. After that, Russell wobbled a bit from side to side when he rode the bike. But he was still able to keep his balance.

"When are you going to take the training wheels off your bike?" Nora asked him.

"I like them," Russell insisted. Teddy had his seventh birthday. Now that he was older than Russell again, Russell didn't feel that he had to be able to do everything that Teddy did. Probably by the time he was seven, he wouldn't use training wheels, either.

"Are you still using those baby training wheels?" Eugene Spencer called out.

Russell pretended that he didn't hear. He pedaled faster than ever. His feet never came off the pedals now, and his leg muscles were stronger and stronger.

At the fountain Russell stopped riding and got off his bike. He took a big drink of water. "Wait for me," Teddy called as he got off his bike and took a drink, too.

The two boys got on their bikes again and rode off together. "I bet you could ride without those training wheels," Teddy told him.

"I don't care," said Russell. "I like training wheels. They help me balance."

Some big boys were playing a game of soccer in the ball field. "Let's watch," said Teddy, getting off his bike. He rested it against the park bench.

Russell got off his bike and put it next to Teddy's. Then he sat down on the ground next to his friend. The big boys kicked the ball and chased each other. It was fun to watch them. After a while Teddy said, "I hear the ice-cream man."

Russell listened. He could hear the bell of the ice-cream truck, too.

"Race you back," called Teddy.

Russell grabbed his bike and got on fast. He pushed off and pedaled as fast as he could.

"Hey. Wait up," Teddy called to him.

"I'm going to beat you," Russell shouted, racing ahead of Teddy.

"Hey, you're riding my bike," Teddy yelled.

Russell looked at the handlebars of the bike. The special horn that he had gotten for his birthday wasn't on them. He was riding Teddy's bike. He was riding without training wheels. He was so surprised that he almost lost his balance, but he didn't.

"I did it. I did it," he shouted as he narrowly

avoided crashing into a bench. He wished that he had his horn because he wanted to make a lot of noise. He wanted everyone to look at him.

"Look at Russell," Teddy called to their mothers, who were sitting together on one of the park benches. "He's riding my bike."

"It doesn't matter," said Mrs. Resnick. "You both have the same bike."

"But mine doesn't have training wheels," Teddy explained.

Russell thought he would burst with excitement. He had ridden a bike with only two wheels.

He was so excited that he forgot that the ice-cream truck was there.

"Come on," Teddy called. "Let's get some ice cream."

"I don't want any," said Russell. "Can I ride your bike while you're eating?"

"Are you all right?" asked Mrs. Michaels, reaching out to feel his forehead. "I never heard you turn down ice cream before."

"Yes," shouted Russell, wobbling off on Teddy's two-wheel bike. "I'm terrific."

He could ride like a real big boy now. He was so full of happiness that there was no room inside him for ice cream, too. He was catching up with Teddy, after all.

By Johanna Hurwitz